Cover design: Aman Raghav
Editor: Ishika Gupta

Poetsandwriters Publishing House
New Delhi, India

For more Information, contact **Aman Raghav**
(www.instagram.com/_amanraghav_)
(www.facebook.com/itsamanraghav)
(amanraghav682@gmail.com)

Dedicated to all the women in my life who have taught me a lot about life, who have helped me to become a better person every single day. Especially my mother- Kiran Raghav and my sisters- Anamika and Ritika Raghav

this is not a poetry book
i have put my heart in your hands
through this
read it again and again
but carry it with care

she sees her chaos as magic
and paints the empty canvas
so perfectly with her
shivering hands
that they fall in love with
her flaws

she listens to songs that
define her in a way no one
else can
you can tell about her mood
by the songs she is listening to

she has a painful past
but she doesn't want to live in it
she wants a rich present with someone
who can love her like no one ever did
make her present so bright
that she forgets about the empty darkness
she has once lived in
kiss her so hard
that she forgets about the dried lips
look into her tired eyes
and make promises without words
hold her hands on her tough days
she deserves an everlasting love
be that love

do not make her go
by your actions that don't match
your empty words
once gone
she doesn't look back
you can fill the oceans with your tears
but she cannot be drowned in it
give her your selfless love
take care of her soul
and she is yours

she loved you but you left
but do not think that she is alone now
even before you came
she was complete in herself
she knows how to handle her beautiful life
you were just a chapter
don't consider yourself a complete story
wake up

when she smiles
even the stars fall for her

she has even made the sun shy with her smile

she has made a home for herself
with her confidence
where she lives happily
her heart is not full of guilt
but compassion
don't come back to ruin
her beautiful home

you will admire the strong girl
she is becoming
leaving all her doubts behind
the kind of girls you find walking confidently
on the roads filled with autumn leaves
the kind of girls who sing madly in cars
as if no one is watching
it took her an eternity
to learn about self-love
you cannot take it away from her

girl
do not care about your ordinary face
there is a boy
who loves your soul
your naked truths
and your half-closed eyes
when you smile
there are people who see you as inspiration
for how you turn dust into gold
with your magical touch
your generousity is your beautiful
do not fall for an ordinary boy
fall for someone who knows
what beautiful is

do not be afraid of darkness
you carry a light with yourself wherever
you go
you don't know
how many lives you have lightened up
with your presence

she doesn't allow anyone to
come in her dreams
for she has kept that place reserved
for someone
who will not be afraid to tell the world
that he belongs to her
that she belongs to him

her courage lies in the fact
that she can be madly in love with you
still
she won't text you
if you are toxic to her
she knows the difference between
right and wrong

girl
it is not your job
to carry the weights of their sins
to make them happy whenever they are sad
to give all of you to them
when you are not feeling good
to satisfy their lust in the name of love
to cry for those who don't value you
girl
your job is
to keep yourself happy
to stay hydrated
to stay healthy
give your life to yourself

she likes poetry
she likes stories
but she won't fall for
your words
she knows the difference
between words and actions
-stay loyal to her

she kept begging for love
from those who only knew
how to break a heart
until she started to love herself
she now knows how to remain
happy in her own company
if she can do it
you can do it too

her definition of love
is different from yours
she finds love
in the eyes that take
care of her
in the voice that makes
her laugh
in the poetry that soothes
her soul
in everything that helps
her to rise

it is not her weakness
but love
if she has returned
after a fight
it is her strength
that teaches her
to forgive so easily

you have known her for so long
you think you know her
but she hides herself
behind her smile
the right one can hear the
pain in the sound of her
laughter
the real one can feel the
crave for someone to touch
her soul without touching her
if she hasn't cried her heart out
before you
don't say you know her

she is like the moon
beautiful and full of flaws
there are days when she
hides herself from the world
but when she smiles
she lightens the whole world
even the sun falls for her

do not touch her body
if you haven't touched her soul yet

but my dear friend
when you keep a bird in the cage
she doesn't love you
she only pretends to be yours
until she gets the chance to fly away
love seeks freedom

for the words will fade
and the beauty will be long gone
what remains in the end
is the endless love
that refuses to go with time
with age
she can give you that love

her scars are gone
she doesn't wear the same
skin as she used to
everything that once made
her sad is gone
including your memories

she is not made of honey
not everyone will like her
she is bitter and sour
once tasted
she can never be forgotten

come to her
in pieces
she will heal you

they call her an artist
but no
she is an art
perfect and priceless
made with patience and love
she always likes the rising sun
she is an optimist and
believes in tomorrows
you cannot break her
she is strong enough to take
care of herself

she is the cold fire
an unsaid poetry
and a beautiful art
she can heal you with
her cold touch or destroy
with fire in her eyes
try to keep her cool

with words so soft
she speaks
and her eyes so deep
i drown

her heart is not a place
that you can often visit
after getting bored
if you can't make it
your home
don't come uninvited

reveal your scars
and be proud of them
they don't make you weak
cowards don't get
hurt in wars
they run

she didn't fall for looks
she fell for the smile
and the eyes that had
a thousand stories hidden

she is enough in herself
a goddess
she doesn't need you
to complete her
she wants you as
someone she can love
and can get the love in return
if you can't do that
stay away

your tears are precious than
the diamond
stop wasting them on cheap
people

never take her silence
as her weakness
there can be a hurricane
hidden behind her silence
and you won't even know

smile whenever you have time
and if you are too busy
find time to smile
this is the gift you give to people
around you
this is the gift you give to yourself

girls like you are the moon
only ocean can kiss you

The person you once believed to be the love of your life will often bring chaos to your mind. I hope you won't hate yourself when it happens. There will be times when there will be guilt, self-doubts, and thoughts of self-destruction. I hope you won't allow them to define you as a person. I hope you won't isolate yourself from the people who want to be there for you.

While the majority of your life that was surrounded by that person will appear to be empty now. I hope you won't stop yourself from looking out for hope, self-love, and new life. There will be an urge to detach yourself from everything. I hope you won't start hating everything that matters to you.

Your life is the sum of everyone you have shared your thoughts, time, and dreams with. I hope you will take everything positive out of that person. The past always feels to be decorated when we look at it from a distance. This often creates a low feeling and we try to find ourselves in the past. I hope you will accept yourself in the present. I hope you will smile.

Talking about harmony and nature, I have seen your eyes shining and your heart singing a sweet melody about the youth years of love. I have engraved the hymns of that holy song in the corner of my heart where I don't allow anyone to enter. The other parts of my heart are jealous of the lyrical beauty that makes the moon dancing.

The oceans are very silent today. There is melancholy. And I have taken you to sing a song for the oceans.

you cannot cut her wing
in the name of love
and ask her not to fly
your love should give
her freedom

there are no excuses for breaking a heart

you call yourself a sinner proudly
and laugh
telling your friends about the secrets
she shared with you
under the moonlight when you told
her to trust you
she cries while you are looking for
another girl
don't worry about her
she will heal herself
    -you belong to hell

The hours of the waiting and wandering of what the stars confess to the sky. The moon and the dim starlight and you humming to a distant song that carries a soothing aura to kiss my cheeks. I touch my heart and it's in harmony. I turn to look at you dancing at midnight. And I wonder of all the promises I have kept. And I know why I am blessed to such moments.

there are people who won't
return your love
it doesn't mean that you
should stop loving
your love is a ray of hope
it brings you peace
you are capable enough to
decide what you want
do not wait for others to return
your love to spread happiness
go change the world

anger shows everything,
it is the smile that hides a thousand lies.

cry
cry your heart out
it doesn't make you weak
cry if it makes you feel better
you are important
the world can judge
don't care about it

I hope you realize that your importance doesn't depend on how people treat you. I hope you realize that you can be happy without any external factors. Your heart is capable of healing if you give it some time. You are rare. I hope you love yourself. I hope before trying to be someone's priority, you are your own priority.

She is the girl who loves the sky and moon more than anything else. The rain gives her vibes. She can sit quietly on a rooftop looking at the clear sky. She is happy with her thoughts. She doesn't need anything to be happy but nature. She likes to read books. She doesn't like kindle. She is a mountain person.

She doesn't care about modern love. She is an old school. She only thinks of the person she loves. There are no doubts about her love. Being in love, she is clear of her feelings. She is honest about everything she feels and she says. There is no comparison of her love. You can find her smiling alone thinking about her lover.

She likes music. Her taste in music is different. She doesn't like the mainstream noisy songs. She calms her mind with music. She likes to walk on empty roads. She likes to look at the stars. She finds the handwritten letters better than the texts.

She looks at the soul of a person. She is not judgemental of your looks or anything else. She closes her eyes when she smiles and it is so cute. She talks with enthusiasm. She falls for the smile and the eyes that contain a thousand stories.

Her childish smile is the most wonderful thing you can ever find. She asks a lot of stupid questions too. You have to handle her on her bad days. There will be days when she will push you away. You have to take care of her with love. She doesn't want anything from you but love. Love her and she will make you the happiest person. Do not ever let go of her.

It is rarely talked about but I want to talk about it. Whenever you will ask for advice, they will ask you to let it go as if it is so easy. I want to talk about the efforts it takes to let someone go.

It takes every bit of us to decide that we are going to give up on the person we love the most. I will not talk about the situations that lead a relationship to its end. It is scary to even imagine living a life that we have dreamed of living with someone. It is so difficult to imagine it without that person. These are the situations of a dilemma when you don't see clearly what is right for you.

Sometimes, we don't get the chance to choose. We are left with no choice. They leave us in the middle of nowhere. This is when we hear from everyone to stop worrying and just let it go. "Take a deep breath, and let it go." As if we don't know it already. But what about the heart that is bleeding. What about the memories that are haunting us every night. What about the broken dream?

It takes years of pain. Missing them becomes a part of our lives. It hurts. It is a gradual process. It is easier said than done. Forgiving is easy, forgetting isn't. We can do everything that is in our hands. We can stop stalking them, we can stop looking at their pictures, we can delete the number and chats. But the heart wants what it wants. We cannot stop ourselves from missing them in the middle of the night. We cannot stop ourselves from dreaming about the time when everything was all right.

Only hope helps us at that time. Only the belief in ourselves. I agree that it is not easy, but it is not impossible. And just because it is tough, it doesn't become a bad choice. You took the right steps. You can do it. You are not alone. I am always with you. My heart goes to you. Trust yourself.

There are nights when she'll ask you to go, when she will be the most vulnerable, when she will try her best to push you away, those are the nights when you have to hold her most tightly, when you have to tell her that you love her in every situation, those are the nights when you have to make her believe that she is not alone at her darkest, that she has found her soulmate. Those are the nights that make a relationship strong.

Love is not only about being together when there is happiness all around. Love is about taking care of her when she cannot take care of herself. Love is about holding her hand when she asks you to leave. Love is deep.

there is no past,
only lessons.

This is me, trying to adjust in a world I don't belong to. I am a mountain person, the one who likes peace and the smell of a new book. So, when they ask me to read on Kindle, I only smile. I value relations so much that even when my distant friend leaves, I almost cry. So sometimes, I feel stuck in a world where they refer to people like us as old-school.

I read poetry as if I have created it, or as if it were created for me. Poetry runs in my veins with my blood, so when they try to differentiate between art and life, I only smile. What is life if it is not given to art and what is art if it does not contain life? Poetry is above all, poetry is art. It is not about the words or rhyming but the aura that it holds in itself, the emotions it carries, the peace it gives to a heart that is still living in the era where it was all slow- the life.

I am often asked to write on a typewriter or something digital, "Diary takes more time," they often argue. I am often asked to reply on time. I am often asked to adjust to technology. But they do not understand that I do not belong here. I am not the person who goes to sunset and only clicks pic, I try to embrace the view, to quench my soul. I like to sit there with no electric device, to wait for the stars to come, to remain in the moonlight for as long as I can before the sun comes again.

So, if you find me sitting in a corner doing nothing, do not disturb me for I like to sit with myself as often as I can.

She is a girl,
A girl of values,
A girl of honours.

She has her secrets,
She has met demons,
But when you meet her,
You get an unbroken smile.

She has loved,
She has a broken heart,
But when you meet her,
You find hope in her brownish eyes,
And when she loves,
She still loves with full heart.

She is so pretty,
She has hidden scars,
But when you meet her,
You like her because of her generosity.

She has been loved,
She has been betrayed,
She has seen nothing but negativity,
But when she talks,
She talks of possibilities.

She feels alone,
Deep inside she is afraid,
But when you meet her,
You admire her for her courage.

Yeah, she exist,
The imperfectly perfect Girl.

it is better to be in love without a relationship
than to be in a relationship without any love

silly girl,
your heart is fragile
but the power is in your hands
do no give it to someone who does
not knows how to handle it

There will be days when she will heal you with her words, with her voice. When you will be craving for her presence, she will do everything she can to make you feel special. Her heart is made of pure gold, she has the perfect soul that can feel your pain even when you don't tell her about it. Stay close to her to feel heaven.

in every falling apart
the heart becomes stronger

she shines the
brightest
when it's dark

like the moon
you can only admire her

it won't be the first kiss
that you would never forget
it would be the last hug
that won't let you sleep

Take your time. Take your time to heal. Everyone is different, everyone feels differently, it's okay if you are taking too much time to heal, but trust me, eventually, you will. Don't allow them to tell you that you are vulnerable because you aren't, you just feel everything in a different way and it's completely fine, don't try to make them understand because they won't. Don't expect them to hold your hands in this journey because most people leave in tough times, hold the hand of those who stay, who care for you, who do not see you as a mess but as someone who is growing, who is evolving. Your beautiful heart is your strength, the way you feel about others is what makes you stand differently from everyone, and if you have to stand there alone for some time, don't be afraid for the night gets dark before the sun rises and the night is not afraid of anything, it stays there. You are strong, don't wait for any validation.

this pain that you are facing these days is only making you stronger. whenever you get time, think about the growth you have achieved during these days of struggle, how as a person you are becoming someone who is not only aware of what she should do but is also aware of the environment that she wants to live in. now, you are choosing your life all by yourself. everyone who used to tell you to change yourself according to them has gone and now it's you with your dreams and a stronger heart that is soft enough to feel everything but is strong enough to tell people to stay away from it if they cannot take care of it.

she was a broken soul
but she never stopped searching
for light
until she found it

how hard is it to let go
of something you wanted the most
how liberating is it to let go
of something you wanted the most
but was toxic to you

in my dream
you were no longer a dream
and it was the best dream
i have ever had

before
we rise,
we fall

don't expect kindness from
the people
who aren't kind to themselves

her smile hides a thousand lies
her eyes reveal them all

only if
all endings
could be as
beautiful as
sunset

and we often want a rainbow
but when it rains, we shut the
doors and windows.
everything needs patience,
you cannot see a rainbow
without a little rain.

i didn't fall for looks
i fell for the smile
and the eyes that had
a thousand stories hidden

I know you don't feel right about love. For you have suffered a lot. You have given everything that you had, and in return, you didn't get anything. At least you tried, you were loyal, don't let those cheap or whatever monsters kill your innocence, or your life, or your hope, or your excitement, or your emotions. Stand up, heal that broken heart, it's yours, they are nowhere close to you to see that, it's you who are struggling. Rise.
All the best.

Some stories are much more realistic than those fairy tales where love is described as 'perfect'. They are not to be shared, but to be kept hidden, deep inside the heart. They have no endings, you just keep scribing them. They are not full of fancy words and clichés; just hope, faith, and love. They are written word by word, with a break after each sentence.

Everyone has that one story, that one forever. They know how to hide that story behind a smile, but you can read it from their eyes.

Look into their eyes. ♥

Just because things once messed up a little, and they were not there for you when you needed them the most, don't stop trusting, don't lose hope; humanity is still alive.

Things are like that, they mess up at times, but it doesn't mean it's always their mistake; circumstances play an important role sometimes. Even if it was their mistake, trust me everyone is unique, they were not for you, move on.

But don't stop loving, it's the only thing that separates us from other living beings. Don't let compassion die. This world is full of love, find your worth.

let this
end be
a new
start
for you

Hello, everyone. This is Aman Raghav. I have written this book with so much love and hope. I hope you loved this.

You can find me on Instagram: @_amanraghav_ Drop your kind messages there. I am waiting.

Printed in Great Britain
by Amazon

49244991R00054